LITTLE MISS HELPFUL
at the Fair

Roger Hargreaves

MR. MEN   **LITTLE MISS**

MR. MEN™ LITTLE MISS™ © THOIP (a Sanrio company)

Little Miss Helpful at the Fair © 2014 THOIP (a Sanrio company)
Printed and published under licence from Price Stern Sloan, Inc., Los Angeles.
First published in France 1997 by Hachette Livre
This edition published in 2015 by Dean, an imprint of Egmont UK Limited,
The Yellow Building, 1 Nicholas Road, London W11 4AN

ISBN 978 0 6035 7131 2
61268/1
Printed in Great Britain

EGMONT

Little Miss Helpful was spending the day at the fair.

I expect you like fairs, don't you? Little Miss Helpful did.

There are so many fun things to do at the fair.

But what Little Miss Helpful liked to do best of all was to help other people, so she looked around the fair for someone who might need her help.

She stopped by Mr Fussy the candy floss seller.
He had a question for her.

"I need to ask for your help, Little Miss Helpful.
Could you look after my stall for a while?
I completely forgot to change my goldfish's water
this morning," he said, "and that will never do."

"Don't you worry," said Little Miss Helpful.
"I'm happy to help."

A moment later, Little Miss Splendid arrived. She had made a special effort for the fair and was looking particularly splendid.

"Good morning, Little Miss Helpful," she said. "I wish to buy a candy floss to match the colour of my hat. It's such a stylish hat, don't you agree?"

"Happy to help," said Little Miss Helpful.

She pressed the button to switch the candy floss machine on.

BRRR!

The candy floss grew, and grew, and grew like a big pink cloud.

But the cloud was getting too big for the machine. It puffed out over the edges and …

Little Miss Splendid found herself completely covered in sticky, pink candy floss.

She was not pleased. Her hat was ruined.

She was not pleased at all.

"Oh, I am so terribly sorry," said Little Miss Helpful. And in a terrible state of confusion she ran away, leaving poor Little Miss Splendid more stuck up than ever before!

Next, Little Miss Helpful went to the shooting gallery.

Little Miss Helpful at the shooting gallery?

That doesn't sound like a very good idea, does it?

I think there might be another problem before too long.

But at that moment Little Miss Helpful noticed a very strange sight indeed.

Mr Lazy, the balloon seller, had fallen asleep.

Mr Lazy had not only fallen asleep but he had also floated up into the sky, no doubt dreaming beautiful blue-sky dreams!

But his dreams would soon be over! Little Miss Helpful didn't hesitate for a second. She picked up an air rifle and …

Pow! Pow! Pow!

Pop! Pop! Pop!

One by one Mr Lazy's colourful balloons popped.

Pop! Pop! Pop!

For once, Mr Lazy was wide awake!

There was a big crash.

Mr Lazy had fallen to the ground, thanks to the help of Little Miss Helpful.

She had only wanted to help, but look what had happened.

Poor Mr Lazy went home, rubbing his poor bruised bottom.

To cheer herself up, Little Miss Helpful went to the food stall. All the best cooks in town had prepared food for the fair.

"Go and get me some bowls and cups, Little Miss Helpful," ordered Little Miss Bossy. "And I hope that, for once, you won't cause any trouble."

But of course Little Miss Helpful wanted to be as helpful as she possibly could, so she decided to carry as many bowls and cups as she possibly could. Well, couldn't, in fact …

The huge pile of cups and bowls wobbled this way and that. It was tipping dangerously.

"Where are those bowls?" asked Little Miss Bossy, impatiently. "What on earth is going on? I didn't ask you to do a dance as well!"

Poor Little Miss Helpful was finding it so hard to keep her balance, she was dancing this way and that trying to keep everything from landing in a heap on the floor!

But alas, one bowl, two bowls, ten bowls … all the bowls and cups tumbled down around Little Miss Bossy and broke into a thousand pieces.

And who do you think landed in the middle of the table with all the food?

Little Miss Helpful, of course.

"Yumm, that's the best potato salad I've ever tasted," said Little Miss Helpful. "You must give me the recipe."

Everyone burst out laughing, even Little Miss Bossy.

And what do you think was the most popular attraction at the fair that day?

Why, Little Miss Helpful's cups and bowls dancing act, of course!